Tales

The Fox
and the Crow

Retold by Diane Marwood

Illustrated by Barbara Nascimbeni

Crabtree Publishing Company
www.crabtreebooks.com
1-800-387-7650

PMB 59051, 350 Fifth Ave.
59th Floor,
New York, NY 10118

616 Welland Ave.
St. Catharines, ON
L2M 5V6

Published by Crabtree Publishing in 2012
Printed in the U.S.A./052012/FA20120413

Series editor: Jackie Hamley
Editor: Kathy Middleton
Proofreader: Reagan Miller
Series advisor: Dr. Hilary Minns
Series designer: Peter Scoulding
Print and Production coordinator:
   Katherine Berti

Text © Franklin Watts 2009
Illustration © Barbara Nascimbeni 2009

The rights of Diane Marwood
to be identified as the author
and Barbara Nascimbeni as the
illustrator of this Work have
been asserted.

First published in 2009
by Franklin Watts
(A division of Hachette
Children's Books)

**Library and Archives Canada
Cataloguing in Publication**

Marwood, Diane
      The fox and the crow / retold by Diane
Marwood ; illustrated by Barbara Nascimbeni.

(Tadpoles: tales)
Issued also in electronic format.
ISBN 978-0-7787-7892-9 (bound).--
ISBN 978-0-7787-7904-9 (pbk.)

      1. Foxes--Juvenile literature. 2. Crows--Juvenile
fiction. I. Nascimbeni, Barbara II. Title. III. Series:
Tadpoles (St. Catharines, Ont.). Tales

PZ8.2.M37Fo 2012   j398.24'529775   C2012-902481-3

**Library of Congress
Cataloging-in-Publication Data**

CIP available at Library of Congress

This kind of story is called a fable. It was written by a Greek author called Aesop over 2,500 years ago. Fables are stories that can teach something. Can you figure out what the lesson in this fable is?

One day, Crow sat in a tree holding some food in her beak.

Fox saw her, and he wanted the food.

He thought of a
clever way to get it.

"How beautiful you are, Crow!" he called loudly.

9

"If your voice was as beautiful as you are, you would be the Queen of Birds."

Crow had always thought she was beautiful.

She thought her voice
was beautiful, too,
so she cawed loudly.

The food fell out
of her beak...

...and Fox gobbled it up!

"Silly Crow!"
laughed Fox.

21

Puzzle Time!

a

b

c

d

e

f

Put these pictures in the right order and tell the story!

vain

sly

silly

clever

Which words describe Crow
and which describe Fox?

Turn the page for the answers!

Notes for adults

TADPOLES: TALES are structured for emergent readers. The books may also be used for read-alouds or shared reading with young children.

The Fox and the Crow is based on a classic fable by Aesop. Aesop's fables teach important principles about greed, patience, perseverance, and other character traits. Fables are a key type of literary text found in the Common Core State Standards.

IF YOU ARE READING THIS BOOK WITH A CHILD, HERE ARE A FEW SUGGESTIONS:

1. Make reading fun! Choose a time to read when you and the child are relaxed and have time to share the story.
2. Set a purpose for reading by explaining to the child that each of Aesop's fables teach a lesson. This information will help the reader understand the story and the features of the genre.
3. Encourage the child to reread the story and to retell it using his or her own words. Invite the child to use the illustrations as a guide.
4. Discuss the lesson of the story. Is the lesson important? Why or why not?
5. Give praise! Children learn best in a positive environment.

HERE ARE OTHER TITLES FROM TADPOLES: TALES FOR YOU TO ENJOY:

How the Camel got his Hump	978-0-7787-7888-2 RLB	978-0-7787-7900-1 PB
How the Elephant got its Trunk	978-0-7787-7891-2 RLB	978-0-7787-7903-2 PB
The Ant and the Grasshopper	978-0-7787-7889-9 RLB	978-0-7787-7901-8 PB
The Boy who cried Wolf	978-0-7787-7890-5 RLB	978-0-7787-7902-5 PB
The Lion and the Mouse	978-0-7787-7893-6 RLB	978-0-7787-7905-6 PB

VISIT WWW.CRABTREEBOOKS.COM FOR OTHER CRABTREE BOOKS.

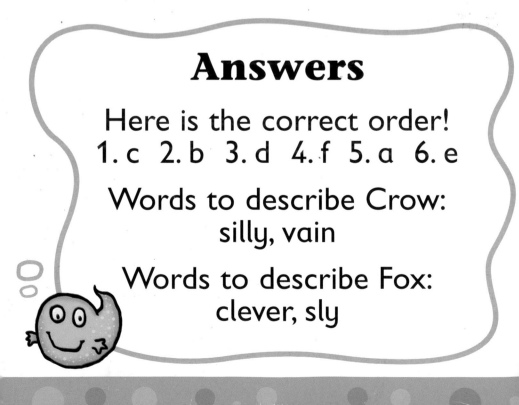

Answers

Here is the correct order!
1. c 2. b 3. d 4. f 5. a 6. e

Words to describe Crow:
silly, vain

Words to describe Fox:
clever, sly